LOVERS

Daniel Arsand

LOVERS

*Translated from the French
by Howard Curtis*

Europa
editions

Europa Editions
214 West 29th Street
New York, N.Y. 10001
www.europaeditions.com
info@europaeditions.com

Copyright © 2008 by Éditions Stock
First Publication 2012 by Europa Editions

Translation by Howard Curtis
Original title: *Des amants*
Translation copyright © 2012 by Europa Editions

Library of Congress Cataloging in Publication Data is available
ISBN 978-1-60945-071-7

Arsand, Daniel
Lovers

Book design by Emanuele Ragnisco
www.mekkanografici.com
On the cover: John Everett Millais, *Chill October* (1870)

Prepress by Grafica Punto Print – Rome

Printed in the USA

To Christel Paris
To Claude Pujade-Renaud
To Bruno and Franck

LOVERS

1

God, how commonplace, in that time before the chaos and the proclamation of liberties, to have a father who tills the soil and a mother who makes invigorating concoctions! It is 1749.

While Alain Faure trudges up and down the fields, panting and sweating, clutching the handle of his plow, growing old before his time, and while his wife Élise feeds the poultry and gathers lemon balm and wormwood, their son Sébastien takes his little flock of goats and ewes out on the moor.

Sébastien is fifteen. A skinny boy with hair like frozen hay. Seemingly placid by nature. A dreamer, a contemplative. Not a common type for a peasant. Anyone with a faraway look in his eyes and his head in the clouds is chastised, forced to perform the hardest tasks, heaped with insults. There are evenings of heavy drinking when some kind souls take a boy of this kind and smear him with excrement, to teach him that reality has a bad smell and you just have to put up with it. If the Devil does not protect him, he will become one of those persecuted people who are found dangling from the end of a rope, encircled by jackdaws. So far, Sébastien Faure has not been covered with shit, has not been the subject of venomous jibes. Thanks no doubt to the terror his mother inspires. Her potions and incantations have made many a strapping lad as soft as chewed tobacco.

He admires Élise, respects her, but, as for loving her, he is not sure, perhaps he does not love her enough for it to really be love. He must be one of those men who are born with a cold heart. After all, being alive does not guarantee having a heart.

2

It is 1749, then, and it is September.

The little flock is idling. It grazes on the short grass between the prickly bushes. The brambles are taking over. They seem constantly on the verge of multiplying, of catching both the shepherd and his animals, and perhaps one day the whole world, in their twining nets.

Sébastien is sitting on a pile of stones, his crook lying across his knees. Here he sits every day, for hours on end, watching over his meager livestock. Boredom makes his brown eyes even more intense. Yet everything distracts him: the breeze that abruptly gives way to a strong wind, the rooks swooping down onto the wild cherry trees behind the pond, the scurrying of a field mouse, the rustling of insect wings. But he is not always fixed in the present. Like everyone else, he has his memories. One of them haunts him: about four months ago he surprised two men in a clearing, their breeches down around their knees, their bodies interlocked. He was a virgin—he still is—and he broke out in a sweat and began trembling all over. At the sight of that scene, he felt both terror and joy. He did not know that this is quite normal when desire becomes too intense.

3

Until he witnessed that eloquent bout of lovemaking he had never conceived of pleasure as anything but solitary, and all flesh had seemed neutral. Since the scene in the clearing, he has been ogling the boys in his village. He is a hunter tormented by illusions.

4

The wind and the rooks have fallen silent. Sébastien becomes aware of a strange silence throbbing around him, broken suddenly by the galloping of a horse. And there it is, emerging from the broom. Its rider is yelling curses. The mare only slows down when it comes to a muddy stretch. It wades into the mire, sinks into it a little, tries to extricate itself, fails, and panics, unseating its master. Sébastien is stunned into silence. So, even a baron, a duke or a prince can end up in the mud? The stained-glass window is shattered. Three more riders emerge from the tall undergrowth. They dismount, they wade, they curse, they bend over the first man, who is gasping for breath.

Balthazar?

Three young men make the acquaintance of fear, even terror.

Alain de Saint-Polgues, Laurent d'Esparres, Anne de Rivefranche—strange boys, rough but precious, not averse to tenderness. Just like Balthazar de Créon, the fourth member of the group, who is lying there with his eyes closed.

5

Sébastien abandons his rustic stone seat and sets off in the direction of the supine figure, filled with the irrepressible desire to touch him, feel him, sound his chest. Resuscitation, he tells himself, is a man's business. He creeps up to the group and slips lightly between these gentlemen with their plumed tricornes.

Who are you?

Hands, arms—or claws. There is a flurry of movement, and the young fops stop him, pin him down with their bodies and their voices. He does not try to escape, for that would mean leaving the injured—or apparently injured—man alone. Instead, he talks to them. The leather bag tied to his waist conceals a treasure, some dried plants, the smell of which is enough to wake a dead man. They snigger, then argue, then resign themselves: let him prove the effectiveness of these plants, or they will beat him. The boy kneels, crushes a small handful of yellowish leaves in his palms until they are reduced to powder, then pours the fragrant dust over the face of the young man, who seems to be asleep.

6

Rainfall can sometimes be miraculous.
There is a flicker of the eyelids, there are sighs and curses. The young man has sat up.

Saint-Polgues places a hand on the shoulder of the shepherd, the sorcerer, the wonderfully placid adolescent.

Thank you, on Créon's behalf.

If Sébastien were not so overcome with the pleasure of having performed a miracle, he in his turn would have uttered an oath and angrily brushed away the insolent paw.

He is the stuff healers are made of, that much is certain, he says it to himself over and over again. And he vows never to find himself, like this man, on a bed of mud. No, never! Not even when he's dead!

He helps Balthazar de Créon to his feet, and when the man leans on his shoulder for a moment, he whispers: I am yours.

7

I am yours.

D'Esparres and Rivefranche bring their friend's mount, which has been grazing under the wild cherry trees. Créon hoists himself up on to his charger as best he can. He throws Sébastien a gold crown. The coin feels warm and soft, it is priceless.

Spurs digging into flanks, whinnying, clods of earth thrown up in all directions: they are gone.

Sheep and goats, broom and heather, short grass and rooks, horses and riders—it is all about to become a memory, and for days Sébastien Faure will have the impression that Balthazar de Créon is the only person who will ever occupy his thoughts.

8

He does not tell his parents what happened that afternoon. In any case, he would not have had the words to describe three strapping young men smelling of musk, a horse trapped in the mud, a prince with soiled garments. How to tell them about Créon?

The crown is buried deep in his leather bag. It must smell of herbs by now.

It is dinnertime. As Sébastien laps up his bowl of soup, his mind wanders. He could never have imagined it was possible to lose oneself in a dream. He is undergoing a transformation. Secretly, he welcomes the coming of night. On the straw mattress he pretends to sleep, letting a powerful silence overwhelm him, a silence of unprecedented happiness. The darkness is the place in which to experience it fully. But when dawn comes, he tells himself that Balthazar was merely passing through his life. He only regains hope by persuading himself that he will have a long, tortuous life, full of chance occurrences. One of these will be a name and a reunion. For one cannot wait indefinitely. He prays to his God for Créon to come back to earth, unaware that it took only a rider, a man lying on the ground, a man resuscitated, for the heavens to become no more than the sky, blue or dark, but forever uninhabited.

I am yours, that was what he said. I am yours.

9

In the fields and on the moor, by the water and along the paths, everything around him is stone. It is as if he is surrounded at all times by something eternal and hostile, while his own inner feelings are undulant, vulnerable, immense, real, unalloyed. The landscape is familiar to him, yet he feels as though he is constantly bumping against it, grazing himself, even breaking his bones, and it makes him dizzy with fear. Until now he has thought that only the body could be hurt. The heart, the soul, those infinite spaces: pipe dreams, his mother has always called them, the fruit of simple minds.

Blinding mineral expanses, precious stones—emerald grass, ruby horizon at evening, amethyst sky.

Sharp stones—flint silence, granite fields, quartz roads.

He waits for the rider's return and some days the waiting is like a madness. It grinds him down, paralyzes him, it is deadly.

He drowns in it.

And Créon does not return.

During the interminable wait, disappointment and sorrow turn to stone.

I am yours. A phrase that leads nowhere, a phrase that radiates sadness, a phrase like a heap of bones.

Winter, then spring, summer, and soon autumn. All seasons are one, ice-cold, featureless, a hell of dreariness.

A year passes, as taut as a bowstring.

One September morning, a coach comes through the village.

10

He is sitting on his usual heap of stones, his crook again across his knees. His animals are grazing. He does not see them. Insects buzz. He does not hear them. The rooks caw. He does not listen to them. The world is on one side and he, Sébastien Faure, on the other, buried, cloistered in his thoughts and daydreams.

And the wind falls silent, and the birds fall silent, and the wild cherry trees no longer shiver and creak.

A horse is galloping nearby, as yet unseen.

The world is again perceptible.

A horse, a rider standing out against the undergrowth, and the rider jumps down from his mount.

I am yours. Sébastien does not even remember that he once uttered those words. He is here and not elsewhere, with no past, no future, nothing to offer.

It is the end of a fine bronze-tinted afternoon with purple shadows and febrile scraps of cloud.

Hello.

11

He gives up his makeshift seat to Balthazar de Créon, and settles at his feet. Each time they meet, and they will meet many times, he will take up the same position. Without preamble, Créon asks him what the beneficial mixture was composed of. Lemon balm, wormwood, mint—these names blossom between them. Balthazar's curiosity is aroused. He demands, gently though, that the shepherd reveal other medicinal secrets. Primrose, chamomile, sage, wild thyme, mallow. Créon marvels at the adolescent's knowledge. He is excited. This boy will be able to keep death at bay.

12

Balthazar is staying with his friend Saint-Polgues, who owns both the moor and the village. The Créon chateau is leagues away. He will return home across the plains, following improbable roads, plunging into the dark forests, but this time it will be an uneventful journey, in other words a safe journey. Because the trees and animals he encounters will be the same as those that surround them now, in this place where they have been meeting for days. There will be nothing out of the ordinary.

They have already met several times. Some of the villagers have seen them in conversation, one man's shoulder resting on the other's thigh, in a kind of embrace. Tongues have started wagging. The Faures are dismayed at having a buggerer as a son. He is regularly whipped, with insults added to the lashes. They scorn their son, although they cannot bring themselves to hate him. They predict that he will burn at the stake one day, as will that ogre Créon, with his powdered hair and satin bow. Those two wretched buggerers should have their throats cut, roars père Faure. Everybody knows Sébastien is seeing that bastard with a noble name every cursed day. Both should be killed, one after the other, but which to kill first?

There will be no killing.

One October evening, the coach with the Créon arms comes to a halt outside the Faures' house. It is as a prince that Balthazar crosses their threshold. Faure yells and screams with anger, with the disgust he feels for sodomites, his humiliation at having fathered one. But his rage subsides as soon as Balthazar puts a heap of gold crowns down between the two of them. During her husband's outburst, and then while the deal is being concluded (Sébastien will live with Créon, everything possible will be done to make him a doctor of renown, he will go to Court, he will treat the King of France—predictions that reduce his father to silence), Élise Faure does not leave the dark corner to which she withdrew when Créon arrived. Henbane, hemlock, digitalis, she mutters. An incantation that no longer works, Elise knows, she has been defeated, and that is something new to her.

I'm ready, says Sébastien.

13

The curtains have been drawn, the seats are padded with cushions, from a basket there wafts a rich smell of roast poultry, fresh bread, and pears.

The coach is a trundling cage, a swaying cradle, a cave.

It is dark and cold. Yes, the trees that line the road are doubtless the same as on Saint-Polgues' property, and so are the animals that loom up out of the darkness, little owls and roe deer, but to Sébastien this world, however familiar, is imbued with a sense of the unknown. In a state of elation, he says farewell to this thing and that, a bridge, a wood, a fallow. What traces will these surroundings leave in him? Do some things sink into oblivion forever? Landscapes, feelings, habits.

14

In calm but unequivocal words (though Sébastien has stopped hearing him: his head nods, his body sags, his eyes close, and he falls asleep), Balthazar ventures declarations, dares to announce what his protégé's future will be, wonders about the indestructibility of all friendship.

You will be my pupil, you will be my master, you will achieve fame, you will be faithful to me, you will abandon me, you will always come back to me.

And at dawn we will say to each other: We are together.

15

Créon will forget nothing of this journey, the only one that will ever truly matter to him.

Amid the reds and silver of the cushions, their silk smelling of chalk, and against the damask covering the window, a fifteen-year-old boy, thin, frail, very frail, but beneath his rough clothes his flesh is warm. A young peasant, a boy exceptionally gifted to feel love. Créon will often tell himself that.

He will never forget the darkness glimpsed through the chinks in the curtains. Soot studded with slivers of moonlight, blackish-brown velvet for league after league. It was deadly boring, and his eyes were constantly drawn back to the confined, shimmering space where his friend was dozing.

He will never forget any of it. But what does that mean exactly? It is vain to believe that one's memory is infallible.

To believe, to hope, to live.

16

Créon's chateau is not far from Moulins. Its gardens are adjacent to a broad, deep forest. Throughout the year, an army of gardeners labors mightily to ensure that the flowerbeds, statues and ornamental lakes are not overrun by tall grass and brambles. Referring to this conquering vegetation, the Princesse de Créon writes to her cousin Angélique de Fombeuse: It watches us, threatens us, soon it will cover the marble.

17

Dear Angélique,
It is a theater of box trees and roses that I gaze upon, but a theater where no actor performs. The audience is unusually restricted, a mother and her son, and a young man forced upon me by Balthazar. When will I see you, my dear?

18

From the terrace that runs the length of the chateau's façade, Anne de Créon watches them. They have jumped down from the coach, and are now coming toward her. It is almost noon. The sun breaks through a sky honeycombed with clouds. Behind Anne de Créon, a tall French door in which her figure is reflected, fragmented by the eighteen panes. That is how Sébastien sees her for the first time and that is why, to him, she will always be two women, a creature of flesh and blood and a shimmering ghost.

Balthazar wrote to his mother: There will be someone with me. I wager that once you set eyes on him you will fall under the spell of my friend Sébastien Faure. In any case, I order you to like him.

Curious, skeptical, horrified, she looks the stranger up and down.

Is this the marvel of whom he spoke? she wonders.

She tells herself again: They are not lovers, I'd stake my life on it. But they are in love.

Anne de Créon accepts defeat.

Welcome to Créon, she says to Sébastien.

19

Immediately upon his arrival, he was installed in a wooden lodge, a kind of chalet, which Balthazar's father Louis de Créon, who died of consumption in 1739, while still in his twenties, had built at the far end of the grounds in order to devote himself undisturbed to the art of the miniature.

The lodge, covered in Virginia creeper and wisteria, consists of two rooms: a bedroom and a study, whose walls are hung with miniatures. They do not depict faces, but apparently idyllic country scenes; only when examined closely do they reveal certain disquieting details: a pond tinged with purple, a hanged man swinging from a branch, an animal choked by a snare, a road obstructed by a mass of fallen rocks, a cutlass driven into a tree trunk. At the foot of the desk are heaps of little canvas bags filled with simples. The hearth is constantly aglow, as there is always some concoction simmering in a pot. The bucolic lair has been transformed into an apothecary's dispensary. Sébastien tests his preparations on the Créons and their servants. Most of the time, the results are convincing. Which gives credence to Balthazar's prediction that sooner or later his friend will becomes the king's doctor. He visits him every day. In the evening, they dine in the chateau, in the company of Anne de Créon. Yesterday, a place was laid for Saint-Polgues, who was passing through on his way to Paris. The conversation was of ancestors and court intrigues. Glittering, uncontroversial chatter, until all at once the Princesse declared that the authority she had once had over her son was on the wane. That cast a chill over the table. They parted soon afterwards. And Sébastien went back to Louis de Créon's miniatures.

20

He has seen the Virginia creeper turn brown, then lose its leaves, he has seen the rain become a daily occurrence, turning the trees and the sand and the flower banks blue or grey, depending on the time of day, he has seen autumn and winter. He has now spent four months in his wooden lodge.

Balthazar always walks him back after dinner. They sit by the fire. There are evenings when Créon says little. A man who keeps silent may touch the emotions. It was during one of the first of these intimate, almost silent sessions that Sébastien discovered how carnal silence may be. Thanks to Créon's silence, he learns to savor the waiting, to imagine what tomorrow will be like, to be silent himself, the better to dream of what is and what will be, of all the possibilities gathered on a threshold still invisible but anticipated. But Créon always takes his leave, always long after midnight. And then the silence that surrounds Sébastien is quite strange, the silence of absence, a silence that drives away sleep. It is possible to lose oneself in it, as in all things.

And tomorrow becomes today.

Balthazar knocks at the door of the chalet a little earlier each afternoon. One of these past days, he declared himself a tutor. He wants Sébastien to learn to read and write, to learn to count, to memorize thankless facts. He teaches him grammar and a smattering of Latin. The pupil is gifted, Balthazar convinces himself; the pupil sometimes expresses his disappointment at some rule or theorem. Is that all it is? he says in surprise. When they go for a walk in the grounds, it is Sébastien's turn to give a name to things and to reveal the daily life of plants and animals. Here is a shrike and here is an oriole, there is the bellflower, there the starflower. It is not unusual for them to venture beyond the gates. With Sébastien, it is impossible to get lost.

Four months, six months, a year.

21

Much to Anne de Créon's displeasure, Balthazar seems to be in no hurry to go back to Versailles. He has been sent for. The King has informed him, through Saint-Polgues, that he is getting impatient. But Balthazar delays his departure. He has even written a brief missive to his monarch, explaining that a strange wasting disease has confined him to his bed. The tone was expeditious, to say the least. It was not well received. He is lying, they say in Versailles, he is handsome and witty but he is a liar. They begin to suspect him of plotting a rebellion, or indulging in some scandalous pleasure, or practicing alchemy. He is a buggerer, they whisper to the King, one who obtains his gold from dark sources. The rumors reach the chateau, the Princesse grows anxious, Balthazar answers his mother's warnings with these words: I am here and they are there. He shrugs, he idles and daydreams, sometimes he even neglects Sébastien and his future. Another day dawns, another night gathers, but he forgets even the passing of time, he forgets that he belongs to this world.

22

God, how commonplace it is to have enemies, how commonplace is naivety, and hatred, and narrow-mindedness, and cowardice, and jealousy, and cunning, and death too, of course, death that comes and goes, a great walker, and madness, and fear, and infatuation. As for love, that is much less commonplace, less than death anyway, but death comes and goes, it is there, it will arise, a distinct event, clearly demarcated, unadorned, death is not a fable. Oh God, how commonplace also are the wind and the rain, the snow, the elements, everything in fact, they too come and go, they come and go but they are not death, not always, they are not its messengers, not always.

And let us not neglect men. Most are insignificant, except them, these two lovers Balthazar de Créon and Sébastien Faure, they are not insignificant, they cannot be, here they are: magnificent.

23

An incurable sodomite, they say of Créon.
Terrible stories circulate about him, at Court, in the countryside, and no doubt in the chateau too.
They surround him like an aura.
Terrifying, but untouchable.
He organizes saturnalia that end in murders, they say.
He is one of the damned.
And as rich as Croesus.
Tall stories, sighs Créon.
He is an ogre, they say.
A tall story, fairy tales, but what is his story?
Who are you, Balthazar de Créon? the local prelate is tempted to ask him.
Nobody can touch him here, on his own lands, he tells his mother.
Anguish is buried deep in his being, silent as yet, but prodigious. It finds expression in an irrepressible need for tenderness. More even than that: in the need to express his desire for Sébastien.
The man they think of as an ogre is a virgin.

24

These days, visitors to the Créon chateau are shown, in what was once the Princesse's salon—no fire in the hearth, no lighted candles—a series of five tapestries depicting the intellectual exchanges between a Greek philosopher and his disciple. Balthazar and Sébastien were the models for these tapestries. The figures do not look at you, they seem absorbed in their own feverish complicity. If you visit this room, which is known as the Lovers' Salon, you will not linger for long. You will feel unwelcome. You will fall silent, and to them your silence is a noise from the outside world. Approach this tapestry, or that one, and when you are close you will become aware of whispers, the rustle of fabrics. You will hear the vows they make each other. It is impossible to take down these tapestries, so it is said. They are in urgent need of restoration, they are a sorry sight, but, so you have been told, it is impossible to take them off the walls. The walls and the tapestries have become one. In ten years, perhaps even earlier, they will fall to pieces, they will be nothing but rags, they will disappear. We will have to rely on photographs for an idea of how those lovers looked. They will vanish, they will be at peace. There will be no farewell.

Miniatures are on display in one of the chateau's boudoirs. Some carry a signature—Louis de Créon—others are unsigned.

The grounds cover a mere tenth of their original area. As for the wooden house, nothing remains of it, and nobody is even sure where exactly it stood. Was it there, where the big pond surrounded by gorse bushes now lies? Or there, on that area of lawn? Or there, where they have built an arbor?

But what are these whispers, this rustle of fabric? The lovers?

25

May the fire and the hate spare us, Anne de Créon writes to her cousin.

The rumors about her son are spreading. From Paris, she is sent lampoons in which he is slandered, branded a seducer of pretty boys, a werewolf, a vampire.

Balthazar shrugs. He is not the kind of person to laugh.

False testimonies are fabricated.

What is true and what is false? Anne wonders.

The Princesse de Créon has a son, and her son is a monster.

Whenever she tries to warn Balthazar, he sends her back to her needlework, sends the titled gossips of Versailles back to their hunts and their balls.

He says: I'm going for a walk. In a wooden lodge is a young man. What they feel for one another has a name.

But what is the world coming to? Anne laments.

Who is untouchable? And who isn't?

She writes less and less frequently to her cousin.

Self-questioning, anxiety, presentiments, a faraway look in her eyes. She is suddenly aware of what quicksand is, and fear, and a gathering storm. Tomorrow is no longer just another day.

26

adame," Balthazar said to her once, "Madame, you are my father's wife, and you are no more allowed to weep than he was. But I, Madame, cannot hold back my tears. They flow sometimes, they are mine, they are precious to me. Why suppress them? I am sure I am like no one else. Not you, in any case, nor my father. Whose son am I, Madame? Tell me that."

What has she passed on to her son?
What does a mother pass on?
She has no idea, no, she has no idea.

Be quiet, she told him.

27

That Balthazar is a sodomite is something she will never get over.

That he is a murderer is something she cannot believe.

That he must end up at the stake makes her love for him all the stronger.

28

They are equals, that is what Balthazar tells his mother, loud and clear. He and Sébastien. One is not the shadow of the other.

He is a sorcerer, Anne de Créon tells herself, this Sébastien is a sorcerer. An exceptional purveyor of narcotics, expectorant syrups, powders to banish ulcers and tumors. Young Faure successfully treats every one of her colds, every one of her fevers. Since he arrived, she has had no aches and pains, she has stopped being obsessed with her own body, she has been in rude health. Now Anne de Créon's one fear is that her son's life will end in flames. But she tries to put her mind at rest: Our young sorcerer will surely come up with a remedy that confers immortality. She clings to the hope that neither time nor man will have any hold over Balthazar, or her, or them, the Créons. There are evenings when Sébastien nods off beside her, in the salon, his thigh against hers. While he dozes, she has the impression that she is moving in pure water, floating in an indestructible, shimmering, reassuringly tangible universe. Sébastien has become part of her life.

29

He cannot stand her. Often during the week, very early in the morning, she sends for him. He has to cross the grounds, climb some steps, must shut himself up in a room with drawn curtains. She is not fully dressed when she receives him. She does not think of him as a man. But he is her present and her future. How much progress has he made with the potion that will guarantee them immortality? He laughs, then says, excitedly: This drug perhaps, and hands her a flask. She drinks the concoction, she knows he is deceiving her, she sends him back to his stills. After leaving her he walks along a corridor, climbs a staircase, knocks at a door.

30

He has reached Balthazar's apartments. He slips a note under the door. One line, no more than that, the name of a place.

The Vauclair Meadow.
Or the Vulcain Grove.
Or the Marcy Clearing.
Or the road to Les Guerdes.
The meeting is arranged. Balthazar has not missed a single one.

31

They stroll beneath the branches, beside a hedge, they cross an area of grazing land.

Sébastien neglects his studies and his inventions.

When their walk is over, there is the chalet, there is the room, there is the bed.

It is now a week since they threw their chastity to the winds.

One day, at the sight of a certain stake, Sébastien will begin to recite, in a low voice, that same sweet litany: The Vauclair Meadow, the Vulcain Grove, the Marcy Clearing, the road to Les Guerdes. An inaudible prayer over the inferno.

32

They are lovers. That is all they want to be. They are at the beginning of their story. Love and passion indistinguishable one from the other.

Yes, he neglects his test tubes and his cauldron.

To paint. He wants to be a painter. But how to depict what dazzles you? So paint a bestiary, paint skies.

Paint the night, the wind, the rain, the stars. And paint the day—blue and gold sometimes.

He asks Balthazar for brushes and pigments.

33

Gently but firmly, Balthazar makes his handsome lover see reason.

He must not desert his laboratory.

Sébastien promises.

He refrains from judging his lover's refusal. For that would mean entering a dangerous area: What does their love consist of? Can one be disappointed and still love?

To paint the night—black with a few streaks of silver.

To grind colors, and then paint.

He decides against repeating his request. And now, whether through weakness or timidity, an obsession takes hold.

To say, "I love you," and feel as if you are dangling over an abyss.

34

He is yielding, he will yield, he has thought it over.
You will be a painter. Like my father.
An austere, reserved man, a hermit, a good man, what more is there to say about him, what more to add, how strange not to be able to describe him more fully.

You will be a painter.

To surrender, to yield to the other's desire, to avoid creating a rift between them, and to think of his father: such a thing has never happened to him before.

35

You gossip. You curse. And then you kill. That is the cruel logic.

What is the exact definition of an abyss, of tragedy, of hell? Anne de Créon writes in her diary.

Since Balthazar refuses to go to Versailles and scotch the rumors, she will go herself.

One morning in November 1751, Anne de Créon climbs into her coach. She will precede her son to Court. She will keep her eyes and ears open, she will judge for herself how much hate there is for her child.

Farewell, make sure you join me soon.

For the first time, the thought of Versailles fills her with panic. Its gardens, its stables, its salons, its bedrooms—a trap, a nightmare, darkness.

36

She has gone, but she lurks, something of her remains. He has never thought so much about her. Absent, she is suddenly real.

Be suspicious of everyone, give up Sébastien, come to Versailles, be my son again, she said to him, shortly before leaving. He fulminates against her voice still echoing around him, endlessly prattling unseen, working hard to turn him away from his love, giving him absurd advice, a fount of common sense and good behavior. He becomes irritable, he is like a caged animal. What to do? He suddenly realizes how much danger he is in. It is possible that he will drag Sébastien down with him, inevitably, he realizes that now. Is he irresponsible? Perhaps. But how to resist certain visions, they will be together, they will experience the flames together.

37

The wall clock in the dark red salon sounds the hours. One hour ties itself to the one that precedes it, and another hooks on to the one that follows it, all with a genuinely glacial indifference.

Yes, it chills the blood.

And so time passes, time spent brooding on grim thoughts.

How many hours does one have to be alive before one can speak of a life?

It is now two years since Balthazar de Créon last set foot on the smallest step of the slightest staircase in Versailles. He is no longer the same as he was then. He is still a prince, but a prince in whom love has been sealed.

Is it really necessary to go all the way to Paris, to Versailles? In her missives, which are filled with information about Versailles and the King, Anne de Créon maintains that it is, with even more energy and pertinence than when she was queen on her lands.

Cut through this heap of nonsense they are saying about you! React! Beg an audience with the King! Do what needs to be done. Am I to believe what they say about you? Think of me, think of your name, think of your dead, do not despise them, do not abandon them.

He writes to her to say that he will go to Versailles. In a week, he and Sébastien will be on the roads. Is she satisfied now?

38

The coach with its high wheels, its well oiled axles, its restored gilt, is like a large insect. It is weighed down with chests and trunks. In a casket are three miniatures wrapped in velvet. These works show promise.

Skulls, a statue, a hat on a bench; corn, a horse, someone—a peasant or a vagabond; a basin, a flight of cranes, an avenue, a tree like no known species. To Sébastien's taste, they ought to be made darker, transforming noon to twilight.

Don't spare the horses, coachman!

The roads are in such a pitiful state, they are constantly thrown against one another.

Balthazar keeps trying to caress his lover, Sébastien's only thoughts are for palette, brushes and paint pots.

Let us never part, Balthazar says, during a halt.

39

Let us never part.
We shall never part.
As in a song that must have already been written.
A song that means nothing.
Nothing. A word of which Sébastien is fond.
Nothing. A word Balthazar rarely utters. The time has not yet come. But it will come, like the rest. And what will the rest be? And the rest of what?
Nothing. Not really, Sébastien tells himself. There is Balthazar. And there is love.

They stop in Roanne, at the Valences mansion, where some distant cousins of the Créons live. There are Créon cousins everywhere in the kingdom of France. Those in Roanne are no more like the Créons than a goose is like a swan. They sleep there one night, one night only. Versailles awaits.
What awaits? Sébastien finds it difficult to imagine his future in the capital.
A nocturnal world, says Balthazar. And darker than this mansion and its paved courtyard, its box trees, its lantern.
Créon's cousins have not expressed any reservation about the obligation to dine with Bathazar's protégé. But once the evening is over, they will gather in alcoves and fume.
At dawn, they set off once more.
They halt here, they halt there: but slowly and surely they are getting closer to Paris.

At the inn of the Green Capon in Melun, Sébastien only has eyes for a kitchen boy with nice buttocks. He will not sleep with him, he will not take the plunge. He loves Balthazar, oh yes, it is love, but his fidelity hangs by a thread. One love, but so many bodies, so many invitations, so many opportunities. Distractions from love. Deep down, he feels alone, and the strange thing is that this solitude does not weigh on him too much. It is acceptable.

Let us never part, Balthazar keeps repeating.

40

The tavern is flea-ridden.

They are lovers, and the vermin are attracted to their bodies. It is a sign of the times.

They have just finished making love, and now Sébastien confesses to Balthazar that he has committed a sacrilege. From the casket, he extracts one of Louis de Créon's miniatures. He has made a corner of it black, soot black. Night appears in broad daylight, through the branches.

Why?

It proves difficult for Balthazar to forgive. Why soil this idyllic landscape? Why darken it? Why? Unless he was trying to emphasize the tormented side of his father's inspiration. And why lose his temper for so little? So little? Sébastien's small sacrilege reveals the kind of man Louis de Créon was, a morose, secretive man, at the mercy of visions. My feelings for him, Balthazar tells himself, my feelings for him, but how to continue, how to describe what I feel for him?

They mistrusted one another, sometimes forgot that they were father and son. And yet, he was his father, a name means something all the same. He has never felt so close to him, which is not much use now.

He will forgive Sébastien his crime, for that is what it was.

My father, the hermit of Créon, he says to Sébastien. And then he kisses his eyes, his mouth, his neck. My beautiful love.

41

Coach, inn, clearing, everywhere they offer themselves, they take and give, without a word, they tune their bodies to one another, after they come they move apart and lie side by side, magnificent lovers, or commonplace lovers, according to preference, and then they start all over again, offering themselves, taking and giving, until the end of time.

42

Hills, plains, mountains, woods, fields, a knoll covered with thickets, herds, farms, then more and more dwellings, a hamlet, a village, dogs, many dogs, in packs or alone, open country right up to the gates of the capital, people, streets, and mud, even more mud than on the roads.

Sébastien leans out the window of the coach.

Will he paint what he sees?

Then he throws himself back on the cushions.

I shall be his patron, Balthazar thinks, I shall confine him to my mansion, he will be mine, just as he was at Créon.

43

He familiarizes himself with the city, sometimes in Balthazar's company, sometimes alone.

Balthazar has not kept the vow he made to keep him prisoner. How could he contemplate such madness? How could he dare deprive this boy of his freedom?

They lunch at the mansion, they dine in taverns. They appreciate silence, but are not averse to getting drunk on noise.

One evening, in one of these places on the edge of the capital, a smoky place stinking of leathery meat that has hung too long and sweat and cheap wine, Balthazar notices at a table near theirs a beautiful young man, lording it over an ill-dressed assembly. This young man ogles Sébastien, and Sébastien returns his glances. Jealousy strikes and wounds worse than a blade, but never, or hardly ever, kills, that is why it is a sister to hate. There is feasting, raised voices, a short distance from them. The beautiful boy is different than the one in the Green Capon, different and the same, but he will be lucky enough to get Sébastien.

I'll be back, I love you.

Betrayal?

Is it?

He loves me, Balthazar de Créon tells himself, it really is love, but he can indulge himself elsewhere, accumulate adventures. All men are alike, except he and Sébastien.

Go, make love, roll about where you want, but don't abandon me.

44

He slipped away with the debauched young man, they went upstairs, took their time, I suppose, and as for me, I left.

And the capital was suddenly alien to me, and the Créon mansion, and my mother watching out for my return, and I waited for Sébastien to return to me, and for everything to be comforting and familiar once again. I was not alone: his absence and our love were with me.

I am Balthazar, Prince de Créon, and this evening I feel a stranger to myself, I feel I know myself less well than I know Sébastien. Is this what it means to experience absolute love, a love from which there is no turning back?

45

He yawns, fully dressed, satin breeches, shirt trimmed with lace, doublet. The beautiful lad has just left him. The room is shrouded in half-light. There is no drape or net curtain at the window. Noises in profusion, voices whining or arguing, there are moans, there is laughter too, and in all this hubbub a strange silence makes its presence felt, it rises like dough between the bed and the walls, everywhere, sovereign and clammy, it paralyzes, weighs on the chest, it is unbearable.

I'm going, Sébastien tells himself.

I'm going. And I betrayed him. The shame and permanence of love, it will be like this for each adventure with one of these brutes picked up in low taverns.

He must learn to play the frivolous, unfaithful role to perfection.

No need to say "I love you" as he slips into bed beside him, he would recognize that body anywhere, he huddles up against him, sinks into sleep.

Sleep, murmurs Sébastien, sleep, my love, sleep, don't ask me any questions, don't say a word, I beg you, stay like that, naked, drowsy, sleep.

46

A good deal of shame, but elation too at discovering that his love for Balthazar remains unshaken. This love will not suffer any change, it has become as necessary to him as breathing, it is his stability, his joy.

And Balthazar forgives everything, Balthazar accepts everything, Balthazar cradles him, Balthazar's presence beside him leads him to sleep and dreams. Thank you.

Three hours with the poorly-dressed man from the tavern, the ogler of boys, the drinker of hooch, three hours of satisfying lovemaking, just three hours and then the realization that it is enough, that boredom sets in once the seed has been spilled and the passion has subsided. Balthazar is once again in his thoughts, his one desire is to see his love again, and all will be well, order will be restored.

They are naked, he and Balthazar, and they feel as though they are floating, lost in each other's warmth, that is their joy.

47

Discreet is the word to describe the Créon mansion on Rue Quincampoix. No atlases, no caryatids. No gates studded like the vault of heaven, no roof surmounted with pinnacles or bristling with arrows. Austerity is the signature. The Créons have always been people who cared more for ideas than decoration. Behind those smooth gray walls, what is brewing? The King has been given evidence that Balthazar transmutes base metal into gold. False testimonies are legion.

Créon will request an interview with the King, although it kills him to do so. What is the master of France to him, when he has Sébastien?

The domestic staff has been reduced to a minimum. A valet, a cook, a chambermaid, a coachman. These four are trustworthy. From father to son and mother to daughter in the Créons' service. As silent as the tomb. Satan's flunkeys, they are nicknamed at Court. They will be beaten, their nails will be teased with iron spikes, they will be thrown into a dungeon and left to rot. They will thus have a glimpse of hell, the eternal dwelling place for queers, it is said.

The princess has dismissed those servants capable, once they are on the street, of chattering about Balthazar and Sébastien and their supposed liking for alchemy and orgies. Yes, the specialists in dusting, brushing and rinsing have been dismissed!

The mansion is like an empty crate. It gathers dust. The walls are coated with grime. It smells like a swamp.

Twenty-nine rooms, only five of them in use.

As for Anne de Créon, she is at Versailles now. She is not allowed to leave. An attic room, like a prison. Every day she confronts the courtiers, once her equals, now her enemies. Let her tongue loosen, let the marble fissure, let the varnish crack, let her betray her son, let what has been kept secret from generation to generation—the taste for alchemy, the passion for orgies, the contacts with sorcerers—be revealed, once for all, and justice be done. But Anne de Créon makes life difficult for those who spy on her, who try to trap her. She is brilliant at evasion. Everyone knows she is mad about her son, Créon the buggerer, the sodomite, doomed to hell. She is dying at Versailles, and the King will not receive her, ignores her during balls.

The Princesse has become a victim.

At last, one morning, the King summons her.

Go, Madame, go to Paris, and bring us back your son.

48

I shan't go. It would be like throwing myself into the lions' den. Not tomorrow, not the day after tomorrow, not ever. Here, in my house, your house, the Créons' house, we know what it means to be silent, what it means to live. I shan't go.

Quiet, my son! This is nothing but lunacy.

I shit on Versailles, Madame, and the King stinks, Madame, oh yes, he stinks worse than ten musketeers. Tomorrow, or the day after tomorrow, one day soon at any rate, I shall go back to Créon. What do I care for the Court and the King, what do I care for your whining, your reproaches, your entreaties?

49

A little more Latin, a little more Greek, a little more French grammar.

Sébastien is more of a dreamer than a good pupil.

He is the angel.

Angel, says Balthazar, angel.

They are together.

How long has the feeling of love existed? Was it born with man? Or did man make it all up?

And who are the barbarians? Is a man who does not believe in love a barbarian?

Angel, says Balthazar.

No more Latin, no more Greek, no more French grammar. Only painting, from now on. There are days when Sébastien shuts his door, even to Balthazar.

50

That blackness in a corner of the miniature was painted with fervor. The blackness that, like a wisp of shadow, is preparing to invade the sky, the trees, the ground. To invade, as love invades all the space, all one's being.

For a time, he will paint no more landscapes, just smears of paint, dark and tumultuous or slow and caressing. He hears them already spreading.

He slaps the paint on.

Or so it seems.

Not only black. A gray monochrome. Sometimes green. Sometimes red.

As he paints, he thinks neither of walls, nor of foliage, nor of blood. He thinks of nothing. He paints what spreads, what colonizes. These smears are alive.

He paints shadows too. Something vague and rumpled. Something that dances slightly, that summons the dusk or the daylight, it is hard to say which.

Even when they are red, in his mind they are always shadows.

Is a shadow silent?

All his life, he may paint nothing but shadows.

And perhaps only faces ravaged by shadows.

Faces beneath which are glimpses of an animal nature, weasel faces, hare faces, fox foxes. Faces out of fables.

But he will never paint Balthazar's shadow. It is too complex, too close to him.

He is afraid that one day that shadow is all he will have left.

It will haunt him.

He does not even give his canvases titles. Can they be called works?

But what does he know of his future, their future?

How can he foresee that he will never paint the dawn, nor Balthazar's shadow, nor the end of time?

51

Sébastien has had several adventures.

His whole body is against mine, Balthazar tells himself, he huddles up to me, he can only fall asleep by my side, he always comes back, but the other man's smell is there, between us, and he does not care, I know, since he is with me, a smell like that is not going to tear us apart, he has told me that, sworn it, he does not lie. But to me, the smell is unbearable. We are different, he and I, why deny it? His is the infidelity, mine the jealousy, ours the undeniable fact of our love.

52

A king is a king, and there are not so many ways to die. There is no point in creating a new one for this Créon, is there? That would be doing too much honor to a sodomite.

He has refused to go to Versailles. And the King is furious.

There is much whispering in the corridors of the palace, many smiles and sneers: Don't you like flames? He does!

This Créon will be executed sooner or later, not because he is a murderer or a maker of gold, nor because of his morals, but because of his indifference to the crown and scepter. Who does he think he is?

Vermin, yes, but as rich as Croesus.

53

Sébastien is possessed. He demands body after body. He wants them all.

And Balthazar says: Enough! And Balthazar says: Ah, here you are at last!

In a notebook, Sébastien writes down measurements, sexual requirements, the duration of each bout, the smells, the quantity of semen, the profusion of body hair on one man, the hairlessness of another, X's profession or Y's flaws, all in a jumble, he reduces these men, these males, to little or nothing.

In a short time, he has established a reputation, one that will last.

He is the Angel.

He is called this by Balthazar, and also by a tavern owner, one of his casual lovers.

There is this tavern, called In the Land of Priapus.

And Balthazar cries: Come back! And Balthazar starts waiting for him.

54

He has dodged all the dangers in which the capital abounds, he deserves his nickname, he is the Angel, it is undeniable.

"Blessed by the gods" would do equally well.

He offers his body to all and sundry, he desires most men, almost all, though some more than others all the same.

He sometimes witnesses brawls, murders, monumental thrashings.

He does not tell Balthazar about his escapades. In their intimacy there is little place for other stories than theirs.

Balthazar implores him to be careful.

What is that tiny boil? That small red patch on the groin?

Is a pox-ridden angel still an angel?

It is nothing, it soon fades, he always emerges unscathed from his nights.

55

He once came close to feeling love for a boy, Christian Guesnes, known as Raging Cock. But a knife in the belly, guts spilling out, and it was all over with the fellow, who was much hated.

There is hate, and that's it. What more to add?

Raging Cock, consummate whore and godlike male at one and the same time, a loyal participant in all the best-attended orgies, Christian Guesnes, the De Broglies' gardener, the man is dead, well and truly dead, mourned by some, forgotten too soon.

Sébastien confesses to Balthazar: I almost fell in love with someone else.

He could leave me, Balthazar tells himself, he could, he can do anything, he is the Angel.

56

Versailles seems to exude a smell of shit.

Créon is done for, they say in the corridors.

Because the King has been told that Balthazar is said to have declared that the Créons are a more ancient line than the Capetians.

The words have hit home. They are repeated. It is like a game of pass the slipper. They are already bleeding their victim dry.

He will be led to the stake, his corpse will be public property, it will belong to everyone, offered to the spectators and to the crows and tiercels.

Tiercel: it was my father who taught me that word.

Be quiet, says Anne de Créon.

Then: Never again venture outside our mansion.

What proof can he give that he is innocent? he wonders all at once, beginning to panic.

He feels homesick for the wooden lodge.

What proof? What innocence?

Oh, my God, and this despair in him.

Don't leave me again, he implores his lover.

Toward what pit is Sébastien dragging him?

57

One evening, the silence in the Créon mansion becomes deafening. It is the lull before the clamors, before sentence is pronounced.

Balthazar, who cannot die, who was not born to die, as they both know, is condemned to death.

My love.

Two little words that Sébastien can no longer bring himself to say, so overwhelmed is he with fear.

He rarely leaves Balthazar now.

What am I still to him, the matchless one? Balthazar asks himself, in torment.

Let me die, before I am abandoned.

But who can affirm anything at all?

Why must fate always have the upper hand?

58

She takes her meals downstairs, in a kind of boudoir, at a richly laid table next to a French door that looks out on a garden no bigger than a pocket handkerchief, green with box trees, a yellow rose bush in one corner. She no longer strolls along the three short paths. If she made up her mind to do so, if she forced herself, she would immediately begin to rail against the world, men and kings, to loathe them. Screaming will be for later. She can only imagine screaming deep in the woods, as she can only conceive of dying in one's own bed, unless one is a man, for any man, as is well known, might meet his fate on a battlefield. Bed or battlefield, but not at the stake.

She imagines the stake, very high and very red, making a noise like a smithy.

Hell on earth—men have been accustomed to it for centuries. She says no to hell.

He must flee.

But Balthazar rejects such cowardice.

No, he will not flee. She despairs of him. Just as he despairs when Sébastien stays out all night, although that happens less often now.

They share a room. Like the poor. They have barred their door to Anne de Créon.

This prohibition has plunged her into a terrible state of somnolence. She is heavy with lethargy. She drags herself along. It is as if she is welded to the marble of her mansion. She shivers. Chaos is nigh.

59

He paints the birth of a shadow. Balthazar's shadow. Managing to do so is a bad omen.

He will leave me the memory of his shadow. Perhaps more. His eyes, the shape of his body, his smell, the sound of his voice. But how to paint them?

I will paint them. I will find a way. I have to find a way. I must be worthy of him. Are we not more than brothers? What can compare with lovers like us?

He has not yet tried depicting the things that fill his memory.

This morning the shadow is coral, this evening it will be golden. A changing, dazzling shadow, but no more than a shadow. There is an eternity between dawn and twilight. And people die.

There is a pounding at the gate. There are cries. The servants are thrust aside. Anne de Créon is manhandled. She screams.

Where are the forests? Where is the wooden house? Where is the night that cradled the Créons' estate?

Today is the day of disaster.

60

She is listening to her voices. There are ten, twenty, a hundred of them, weaving a litany of despair. She talks to herself, and her words are harsh and imperious. Poor girl, are you spineless, are your legs of flannel, have you no guts? Why could you not remove the danger, why could you not persuade them to go into exile, in Spain, Italy, even Canada, over there they would name a city after them, the Créons would rule over the New World, but no, it was beyond you, you moaned, you warned, but ineffectually, being a mother was beyond you, it was as if you were paralyzed, you shriveled, a fossilized dragon, that is what you were, and even today, it was all too much for you, you were unable to be a bastion, an insurmountable barrier, you, Anne de Créon, poor girl, they took your son away, and Sébastien, the boy who made you believe in immortality, bowed to his lover's wishes, do not move, said Balthazar, stay where you are, I beg you, all that love in him, and that insane plea on his lips, and Sébastien did not move, did not intervene between Balthazar and the King's henchmen, haggard, as if dead, paralyzed, they arrested my child, my handsome, irreplaceable child, and young Faure held a miniature in his hands, the portrait of a shadow, he told me, a strange title, to me it was all twisted and seething, with squirts of red, gray, green, it was obscene, they took away Balthazar de Créon, the last of the line, no more heirs, no more eternity, I implore my voices to merge into one, all my voices in one, all of them, for then I would find the words to move mountains, to melt the hearts of all the judges of France and Navarre, they took him from me, they took him away, they will break his bones, and how then will I recognize him?

61

He is thirteen years old, Paris-born, unusually thin, and he is devoted body and soul to his mistress, Anne de Créon. For the past six months, he has been carrying all over Paris the missives she writes at every hour of the day, febrile and trusting. He slips through the streets, like a streak of gray in the light, sometimes melting into the light, he is perfect for this job. She has chosen him as her messenger. He carries letters to such and such a great and honorable personage, all reliable friends of the Princesse, mere scribblings, it is said. He can neither read nor write. But to him these letters are more precious than relics. He would like to keep them. They are burning hot between his skin and the cloth of his shirt. They are calls for help, requests for support, begging letters, so the rumor goes.

The Créon woman, that is what the Princesse is called now.

There are friends who do not dare remain friends.

He will kill them one day. He will always love her.

He will indeed kill a few, later, when the flames of the stake have died down.

A thirteen-year-old monster.

God is no more than a decrepit, senile patriarch, asserts Sébastien Faure, and should be buried in a common grave.

She will never abandon him. To him she is a heavenly creature. She is Madame de Créon.

She will abandon him, though, when her son is dead, when she has become the slave of an irrevocable madness.

He will not kill her. He will kill those who have killed her, the immaculate one.

She will abandon him when she has lost any sense of what it means to live, to abandon, to suffer, to die.

I am the sublime messenger of Anne de Créon.

Yesterday, his name was still Jean Cerneau.

62

Anne de Créon looks to Sébastien for support. She sees her son through him. She cannot get enough of this intimacy, fragile as it is, which a shared despair has established between them. She sees in Sébastien all his love for her son, a mutual love, she sees love itself, she understands what love is.

Tell me about this love.

She addresses him formally now, like a mark of respect. He is her son's beloved.

He always yields to her entreaties. He tells her about their first encounter, how they recognized each other. Then he falls silent. Is what happened next capable of being expressed in words?

She sees love in this young boy, but he will not teach her what love is composed of. He is reluctant to describe its changes, its highs and lows, its very matter.

Every evening she joins him in his room, sits down in the space between the bed and the wall.

Tell me in detail about this love, make an effort, come, love me a little.

He will never go any farther than an account of their meeting.

There are evenings when she is confronted with an empty room, and feels as though she is falling through a trapdoor.

The next day she asks: Where were you?

Nowhere, here and there. Or he does not reply.

He has no hesitation in being rude to her.

There are nights when he lurks outside the prison. He calls out his lover's name, one of those stifled, inaudible cries that rend only the heart. He is almost destroyed by this cry that cannot free itself from his flesh, this cry that is in him, that harrows him, torments him, breaks him. From the vicinity of the prison he heads for a tavern, any tavern. When some strapping lad possesses him, the pain eases, it grows silent, but does not disappear, it cannot disappear, it goes to ground in him, very deep, it is like the sleep of pain, and its silence makes the pleasure incredibly strong. But in the morning the pain is resurgent, and unbearable.

And Anne de Créon is always waiting for him.

She needs him so much, can't he understand that, needs him so much, needs him totally, and at the same time there grows in her a spiraling revulsion, a resentment that overwhelms her: It was Sébastien who brought this anathema down on our heads. He alone is responsible.

Immortal little swine.

63

A man's bedroom is not a woman's bedroom, obviously. The smell is different.

A man's smell is more acrid, more external, less intimate, less secretive, emanating less from within, than a woman's. A smell of sweat and semen, basically.

He deserts his room, he is reluctant to have any more private conversations with Anne de Créon. He hates her, but in him hate is only fleeting, it comes and goes. It is not stable, not binding. A small hate, a hate that does not make a man, some would say.

His smell is everywhere, hovering in the air, impregnating the sheets, and Anne de Créon, in Sébastien's absence, breathes it in deeply. The smell is like her son's, strong and bitter and unforgettable. She lies down on Sébastien's bed, and the illusion is even stronger: her son has slept here, this is his smell. But as soon as she moves away from the bed, she thinks of her child's inevitable death.

64

Where are you? What are you doing? What am I to you at this moment? The one who must be saved? The one who is loved? The one who is nothing but memory now?

He eats little, drinks a few mouthfuls of briny water. He is vegetating. Here, there is no day or night, only shadows. Let there be light! Stuff and nonsense! The hope of the simple-minded. He will leave his cell only for the final torment. It is so dark, he cannot distinguish shadows between himself and the table, himself and the door, himself and the floor. They belong to the outside world. Sébastien clothes them in colors. Indigo, like the evening sky sometimes, fern-green—a dull, almost dusty green—purple, like the rouge on his mother's cheeks, yellow, like straw, or an oriole, or a country path in the summer light.

I think of you.

65

He is suffocating.

Here on earth, one always suffocates a little, for one reason or another, even at moments of great happiness.

He can only live on this earth, even if he is alone. He is of this world and no other.

To die, yes, sometimes he thinks of interrupting the course of his life with poison or a knife, but not before Balthazar has been tied to the stake.

A drastic, suspended, repressed decision.

It is considered good form to hide such a desire. You may think about it, of course, but not commit the act. Suicides are not worthy of a mass.

A man without God.

An unbeliever.

That is what I am, very much so, and forever.

My God! What has become of Balthazar? Are our sufferings comparable? He is condemned to the flames, and I am free.

He is not allowed to visit him.

Balthazar.

Créon.

Him.

The words of a deeply painful song. Three words. The only ones that mean anything in these days of distress.

It has been announced that the trial will begin next week.

The dice will be loaded.

His death, it is said, will be an example. To whom? Is it necessary?

Balthazar.

My love.

And the anger in me, deep inside me.

We are forbidden to meet, to touch, to be again what we have been before, lovers.

We love each other.

Even without touching, we are still lovers.

Will we meet again?

66

I love you.
He writes this little phrase an incalculable number of times in his notebook.

A little phrase so real, it embraces all of reality.

He could even write: I worship you.

Love, worship, what does it matter, nothing really matters, compared with what tomorrow will be, the pain that holds you in its embrace, as no man has ever done.

To love God, to worship men, what does it really matter?

This is a century in which it is rare to say I love you.

He writes the little phrase, murmurs it in the silence.

He is in love.

He loves.

His notes containing nothing but that inflexible little phrase are intercepted, he is sure of it. He never receives any reply. But they still talk, and answer each other, unseen.

He also sent Balthazar a miniature. Light breaking through foliage. And their two shadows merging at the foot of a tree. Here again, not the slightest sign that Balthazar ever received it. Silence, a hell.

I love you, written from the depths of hell.

From there or elsewhere, they are words the other can hear.

Do you hear me, my love? Can you still hear me? What do you hear of me?

The boys he possessed, or who possessed him, are now forgotten.

Don't die.

And Anne de Créon roams her mansion and persists in asking him questions. He has started closing his door to her. Let her die!

Apart from Balthazar, nobody has the right to approach him.

67

One night, he leaves the Créon mansion, never to return. The capital is reduced for him to the few streets close to the prison, a tavern where he dozes without any desire, and a room in the house of Saint-Polgues, the friend who has not turned his back on the Créons, do you remember Saint-Polgues, he came riding across the moor one spring day, and do you remember Balthazar de Créon lying in the mud, surrounded by brambles?

Saint-Polgues intercedes with the King for Créon to receive at least one letter from Sébastien.

He is pugnacious.

He has succeeded.

68

Sébastien Faure has vanished, the taciturn, insolent Sébastien Faure, her son's lover. Fled without a word of explanation. Where is he? What is he up to? Has he been able to reach Balthazar?

She has been refused everything: she cannot look at him, touch him, say to him: My son, she cannot say to him: I'm here, she cannot say to him: Don't speak, let's stay like this, don't speak, she cannot say to him: How are you?

One evening, an idea forms inside her, it is a beautiful idea, an exciting idea.

To feel that she is somebody a while longer.

She sends out invitations to all the nobility of France, invitations to a ball at the Créon mansion. She will be queen of the ball, and while it is in progress she will implore her guests to spare her son the stake.

Even the King has been invited.

She forgets that for weeks everyone has been avoiding her.

There will be thirty thousand candles, heaps of food, dozens and dozens of decanters filled with the finest wines in the kingdom, musicians.

Will the King come?

She is Olympian in her patience, they are taking their time, King and courtiers alike, and she waits, bejeweled, scented, rouged, wrapped in satin and lace, seated in an armchair raised up on a dais, while chaconnes and pavanes are played, it is a long way from Versailles to Paris, she tells herself.

69

The street has not echoed to the rumble of coaches. The King has not come, nor have the courtiers. The night is the color of fire, the candles have already been replaced twice. Thirty thousand candles, that is quite something, is it not?

It is six in the morning, and rather cold, in spite of those thousands of flames.

What season is this?

Her faithful messenger has huddled against her. She cradles him.

They won't come now, she says.

Madame.

I shan't move from here.

Madame.

Are they dead?

Madame.

I shall wait a little longer.

Madame.

And he hums her a lullaby.

70

"Honestly, how could we possibly have gone?"

"Personally, I did think of going."

"You did?"

"Yes, I did. Don't forget, I'm seventeen, I haven't yet witnessed a rout, a shipwreck, for it was indeed to a shipwreck that Madame de Créon summoned us."

"The lights burned late. I know, because one of my servants was keeping watch outside the mansion."

"She is mad, isn't she?"

"Anne de Créon? It seems very likely. The imprisonment of a son is often a source of derangement."

"I thought that kind of derangement was a thing of the past, that it never happened these days."

"The Princesse de Créon, raving mad."

"Who gives a ball."

"To which nobody comes."

"And all for a son. Her own son. Who has been condemned to death."

"Why love a son so much, if it is to see him end up in the hands of the executioner, if it is to lose your reason over it?"

"They say she was magnificently dressed. Ultramarine satin and gilded lace trimmings, it was superb, a touch extravagant, but superb all the same, exactly what was needed to clothe her madness."

"She always did have exquisite taste."

"Is it possible, then, to be both mad and elegant?"

"Apparently."

"Did you know that she makes her coachman stop outside the prison every afternoon?"

"She's constantly leaning out the window."

"What is she hoping? That they will have pity on her?"

"She already has our compassion."

"And that is enough. No need to go farther."

"She is guilty of giving birth to a monster who fears neither God nor man."

"And of loving him."

"And of forgiving him for being what he is."

"Is she—or has she ever been—as immoral as he is?"

"Yes, if we consider her unceasing indulgence toward her offspring."

"Then she does not deserve our compassion."

"Shall we dance?"

"Here comes the King."

71

The time has come for the trial. It will last a week.

The charges against Balthazar de Créon are many: murder, sodomy, holding black masses, practicing alchemy, lèse-majesté, making defamatory remarks against the monarch.

The judges are savoring the fact that at last they can bring this man to his knees, the worst kind of man, a Gilles de Rais crossed with a Fouquet.

They will kill him, they will see him go up in smoke.

Judging the unnamable is a godsend to these people, it will be an imperishable memory, their claim to fame. It is not every day they get to judge a creature of the Devil.

Créon is of no century and of all time, but it is our century that will condemn him.

Will evil be reborn from his ashes?

Is Balthazar de Créon a phoenix?

We shall see.

The one thing certain is that God is in this room, invisible and omnipresent.

The judges are puffed up with pride, there are ten of them, not too many to sustain Créon's gaze.

72

He has appeared to the crowd as they were hoping he would be, thinner, unsteady on his feet.

But there is no sadness or fear in his eyes, they are strikingly, unspeakably serene.

Some in the audience see a resemblance to one of those saints who met a martyr's death. It is embarrassing to think this way, and they will clamor for his head with even more vehemence than their neighbors.

It is a show, a piece of theater.

And when you are at the theater, you do not ask yourself who you are. You clap and whistle.

When he came in, they all held their breaths.

He is so thin, so unsteady on his feet, is he still breathing?

He came in and looked around, at the judges, at all those spectators, at some of his friends, Saint-Polgues and d'Esparres, his mother, his love. A poignant, luminous gaze. He is already in his death throes.

73

She only attended the trial for one day.

She did not recognize him. She barely knew who she was herself. She had forgotten she was a princess, a woman, a mother.

Her young page, her dear messenger, begged her to sit down and she sat.

She had forgotten what it means to be a master or a slave.

To beg or to command, it was all the same to her.

She had forgotten what love is, what hate is, she was alive and she had ceased to be anything.

She complained: I feel hot.

Her page wiped her face with a handkerchief.

She said: All these people!

And her page pulled her by the sleeve and took her away from this cauldron where Balthazar de Créon was the center of attention.

She had forgotten what a farewell is.

74

It is forbidden to stand when you feel like it.

It is forbidden to talk to your neighbor in a loud voice or shout at the condemned man.

It is forbidden to change seats.

It is forbidden to say to the accused: I love you, or anything else like that.

Sébastien Faure stammers out a song. And this song reaches Balthazar. They exchange glances.

Sébastien Faure stares at his lover with all his past and present life.

They look at each other, their eyes wed, they are together again, they embrace amid shadows and voices that are not of their world.

Their bodies converse. They forget that very soon one of them will be burned alive on Place de Grève.

Unless forgetting is an illusion.

But this illusion is their whole reality, it is palpable.

They are as close as two lovers can be.

They no longer even need to say: I love you.

75

The trial has already lasted five days.
There is a proliferation of witnesses.
The Prince makes no attempt to rebut the accusations against him.

The Prince is sometimes bored, that much is clear.

Six days now, and the Prince is yawning.

Vermin, someone yells.

Little children sodomized, then their throats cut.

That is what he is accused of.

The false witnesses have rushed to the stand.

Hired and paid, by whom? The King?

Ogre.

He refuses to answer.

Leave me alone, that is what his eyes say.

He yawns and they insult him.

Monstrous indifference.

Leave me alone.

When will he burn?

76

Sentence is about to be passed.

Créon sways, his hands find no support, he sighs.

I will paint, even without him, Sébastien tells himself, I will paint what he will never see again, what will happen in the future, he will be dead and I will paint.

I will paint our earth and some of its inhabitants, the sly, the cowardly, the envious.

I will paint the sky and I will paint the path that vanishes amid the undergrowth.

I will paint that woman in her fichu and her useless legs.

I will paint the sun and all the stars.

I will paint the night and the animals that come out at night.

I will paint yesterday and I will paint today.

I will paint injustice, violence and hate.

I will paint fairness, peace and love.

I will paint that boy with the narrow hips and flat stomach and pockmarked face, I will paint my desire for him.

I will paint the storm and a cloudless day.

I will paint the newly trampled grass and the moor.

Everything can be painted, my love.

And I will paint death, my love.

77

I was present at your death, I watched it all, and it is as if what I saw and heard has devoured everything within me.

You cried out and I was suddenly blind to the others, to the whole world.

The only things that existed for me were the stake and your cry.

The same cry, repeated over and over behind a curtain of flames. I heard you but could no longer see you.

And all was silence, the roar of the flames and the yells of the crowd.

And the cobblestones, and the houses surrounding the square, and the executioner, and the priest, silence, my love, nothing but silence.

And I realized all at once that I will not be able to paint all that.

I will paint only insignificant things.

It was as if I was formless, weightless, powerless. And I will be that way forever.

That cry he gave!

I heard it. What else could I hear? And for the first time in my life, I hated something of his.

That cry that some call inhuman.

Perhaps because it is the last cry a man can give. It emerges from the last frontier between what is and will no longer be. It is absolutely human, my love.

It is the only cry that you, like all of us, can utter, the only true cry. And it is that cry that I heard.

I will not paint again, my love.

Don't abandon me.

78

You did not have to say: Don't go, come back.
You did not abandon each other.
Apart from this love, its twists and turns, its clarity,
everything is negligible. Unknown men no longer arouse your
curiosity.

That is what provokes your suffering: although Balthazar is
more than your shadow, although he is another you, you can
no longer touch him, it is seeing him that you miss. This love,
however great, will no longer evolve.

You have lost your future.

You no longer wonder how tomorrow will be. And that is
why your contemporaries think you mad. Just like Anne de
Créon. You have learned that her riches, her lands, everything
has been confiscated. By order of the King, she has been confined to a convent for life. You do not care. She is more dead
to you than Balthazar will ever be.

Tonight you tried to draw Balthazar's cry. You could not
do it.

I will not paint again, you told yourself. And you wept.

You will be able to paint nothing now but what is formless.

So you make a bundle of your brushes and pigments and a
notebook on every page of which your beloved is radiant, as he
was before the flames, and, without taking your leave of Saint-
Polgues, good old Saint-Polgues, you flee Paris.

79

The capital is now far behind you.
There is this road, and that one. It makes no difference now, whether you choose to go right or left.
One month, two, three.
Six months.
A year.
He is still alive in you, but as the days pass you hear a new presence throbbing inside you, and this presence is your own, although you no longer recognize yourself, you have been stripped of everything, even your grief.

80

Why did he stop here rather than there? His exhaustion, of which he had ceased to be conscious days earlier, months earlier, suddenly overcame him, urgent, perhaps final.

Sébastien Faure was found looking through the gilded bars of a gate at an avenue, trees, a chateau. He muttered to the people who surrounded him, bent over him, that he was sick with exhaustion. That he couldn't go on, that he was hungry and thirsty, that he was cold, that he was hot, that he could no longer feel his legs, that everything was confused in his head, he spoke in an uninterrupted flood of words.

Suddenly his knees sagged, and he collapsed to the ground, sobbing.

Exhaustion, but not imminent death.

What keeps him alive is a hidden energy, where it comes from, what sustains it, who can say, surely not him, surely not anyone. It sustains him, but for how long? For what purpose? Until what dawn? Until what night? Until the love and the presence that possess him have lost all their splendor, suddenly, and all their stillness, and they disintegrate and collapse, until they are nothing but a memory, the most beautiful and intense of memories, but a memory nonetheless, coming and going in his mind, appearing, disappearing, reappearing, less essential all at once than what dances and sparkles or sheds its flowers, fades and dies around him, the world and its landscapes and its inhabitants.

Come and rest.

A hand on his brow, a little water on his lips, arms that lift him up.

Take me.

81

His rags have been thrown in the fire, he has been deloused, fed, and given a bed in a building where the coachman, the washerwomen and the apprentice gardeners live.

He will be a gardener. The Comtesse de C. has decided.

They are curious to know his story. They press him to tell it. He refuses, then yields.

He will not breathe a word about Balthazar, the miniatures, the stake, or any of those things that are so thoroughly part of him as to be unrepeatable, he will tell them something else, another story. He is still a young man, but he seems older than his age. The cold, the sun, the hunger, the endless walking, the several winters he has been through, have traced small lines on his face. He is as old as his own face.

They learn that he was a painter of no renown—he shows them the brushes and the pigments, now as dry as twigs or as cracked as mud in summer—they learn that he was married, that he had children, that the croup took wife and offspring from him in the space of a few hours, and that since then he has had only the roads and the woods for companions.

They are moved by his story. They like him a lot.

My little gardener, the Comtesse has nicknamed him.

The servant girls are sensitive to his faded beauty. He is tall and broad-shouldered. He is a man. But something stops them from offering him their beds. He lacks desire, that much is clear.

They think they are his friends, as if his confidences have

woven a bond between him and them, but inventing a life was merely a way to make them leave him alone, then and forever, alone with his silence, his grief, the virtue that has been forced on him by misfortune. No one can gain access to him, that is the way it is, and many find his ardent sadness unsettling.

Ten years pass as if they were a day.

He sleeps like an angel. He has forgotten that he was the Angel. He does not dream.

He is an excellent gardener.

He marvels at the splendor of the flowerbed. He is its sorcerer. Tulips, and then roses. The box trees are well pruned. They smell fragrant. After pruning, his body gives off a bitter odor. It is his smell, and has been for a long time.

82

A morning came when the sight of the roses sent him into raptures. That was the morning he realized that Balthazar was losing reality within him. The world existed again. And how good it was!

He did not rebel against the fading of Balthazar. It surprised him a little, then he accepted the joy overwhelming him, a very old joy now suddenly new-minted, buzzing, filled with sunlight. Yes, it was good. And peace entered him.

83

André Francartin has fathered four sons and four daughters, equal numbers, like poor people or ogres in fairy tales. His wife is sly and vivacious. She used to be pretty. She and André live in sweet complicity. It is their daily bread. Their lovemaking is regular and restrained. Julienne Francartin has never had any cause for complaint. Her husband is not a violent man.

André is forty-five years old. He is the Comtesse's chief gardener. He is in charge of a team of six young men, including Sébastien.

The Comtesse often stops to talk with him. There is a kind of friendship between them. But she confides in Francartin neither the vagaries of her private life nor the revulsion she feels for Versailles and the Court, nor does he complain about his children's illnesses or tell her how worried he is about his frequent headaches. In other words, there are no confidences between the two of them, but there is still a certain pleasure in meeting like this in the grounds and talking about seedlings and grafts. She admires him, he respects her.

No sooner did Sébastien join his group and take up the pruning knife, the shears and the adze, than Francartin took him under his wing. More than that: he regarded him as a son.

He has been The Son. No more, no less.

And Balthazar is more distant from Sébastien every day. Unless it is the other way around.

His memory is like quicksand now, or like a desert.

He has grown fond of Francartin.

He will cease to be a son or a gardener or a man obsessed by his past, the morning Francartin stretches on the ground, laid low by a migraine.

Everything is still possible.

84

The scene is apparently bucolic, almost a cliché, frozen in a tranquil sensuousness.

The Marian blue of the sky rejects clouds.

In the lean-to where André has taken shelter, a smell of dust, straw and sweat hangs in the air. The ground is padded with straw. He is sweating abundantly. With one arm he covers his forehead.

He could be a shepherd of Arcady, asleep.

He sighs at regular intervals, a hoarse sigh. Leaning over him, Sébastien fans him with a handful of straw. In his eyes, a strange panic, a supplication. And now those eyes express only desire.

The false shepherd half opens his eyes, the migraine has worn off. He does not say a word of thanks to the man leaning over him. Nor does he make any move to draw him close, but he savors the silence he imposes and the happiness of being looked at.

Sébastien lies down next to him.

85

They graft, they dig, they manure the flowerbeds, they rake, they behave toward each other just as they did yesterday, just as they have always done, they keep a friendly distance, they give away nothing of their newfound intimacy. An observer would have to be unusually perceptive to have any inkling of the bond that now exists between them. They are constrained to wear masks by centuries of repression of male love, and this constraint intensifies the constant desire they feel for each other.

It is all very commonplace, all very unbearable.

Conjugal duties are performed as before, the children are pampered.

By force of circumstance, embraces between the two men are rare.

Nothing is more mortal than a feeling condemned to invisibility.

They sometimes manage to meet in the darkness of a barn. Their nakedness belongs to the dark. It is a humiliating fact. After making love, they await a miracle: to be transported elsewhere, all at once, just like that, they are melancholically happy.

86

Who are you?
They have so little time, so few opportunities, to find out.

They are in love and know so little of each other.

They have just made love. They have stopped talking about a land of light toward which they can sail. Abruptly, Sébastien declares: I lied.

He admits that he was never married, never had children.

He says: I have never had anyone in my life.

He cannot bring himself to utter the name Balthazar de Créon.

For a moment, it seems to him that today, at this hour, this is all he possesses, this lie of omission.

Yes, Balthazar is no more than a memory, but a memory even more powerful than the love he feels for André.

How could he have admitted to André that his love for Balthazar was incomparable, that their own, however genuine, however passionate, is a lesser love and will always remain so. He had never imagined that there could be degrees of love.

I shall paint your face, he says to André.

87

How many years is it that they have been married? The bridal wreath has withered but has not yet turned to dust. Fragile and eternal, it sits enthroned above the hearth. They live in a tiny lodge, a kind of chalet, at the far end of the grounds. The trees are so close, their leaves rustle so loudly, that when the windows are left open you have the impression that an invisible forest is coming to life in the middle of the rooms. The Comtesse long ago granted them this lodge. Her benevolence toward them is measureless.

As soon as spring arrives, the Comtesse grows impatient, she is waiting for a miracle of blooms. André Francartin has never disappointed her.

It is a Sunday afternoon. He and his wife have taken an afternoon nap. He has just possessed her, unhurriedly, with a controlled fervor. That is when Julienne starts to calculate how many years the two of them have been married. Images disrupt the figures. Clear images. Their first kiss, their engagement, the edge of this wood, their first embrace, the births of their children, and the sight of her man in the grounds, surrounded by flowers, and the mad desire she had for him. Clear images, yes, but they end up overlapping, merging, producing a vagueness, a glistening mist that nevertheless evokes happiness, fulfillment, something that endures through, and in spite of, everything. Is it love?

88

She is going to get up, she gets up, it is slightly cold, even in summer, too many trees around the lodge, she has gone to make him a bowl of milk in which she crumbles a slice of bread, he calls it a delicacy, she spoils him, they are no longer in the first flush of youth, the children are married, yes, no longer in the first flush of youth, their teeth are bad and their joints rusty, they make do, they are together, she pours the milk into the bowl, she crumbles the bread, she smiles, and then her smile fades, she realizes that he has not called out to her from the bed, where are you, what are you doing, today he isn't playing at being anxious, where are you, what are you doing, and she starts to wonder, what's happening, why that silence, and fear, a very small fear for now, enters into her, they have possessed one another, they have never said "my love" or "I love you" and yet how to deny that there is love between them, where are you, what are you doing, and it is she who calls out to him those two unimportant phrases, from the depths of their shared life.

89

She knows the bulk of it. He is no longer really with her. She knows that he is abandoning her, even when he possesses her, even when he asks her how her day has been. Even when he says: Come to me, even when he kisses her neck and strokes her hair. She knows and says nothing. She also knows that he will never leave her.

90

He ages all at once. The migraine will not leave him. His inability to come to a decision torments him. To flee, no matter where, he cannot stand it anymore. Sébastien has painted his face on a flat stone. It is a perfect likeness, almost embarrassingly so. He has painted all he has been, all he is, all he is living through, he has painted his joy and his heartbreak.

That's me, he says.

And he runs away.

91

He is betraying her, but with whom? She needs a name, she needs to judge her rival, evaluate her own chances, if she wants her man back. Twenty-nine women live in the chateau and its outbuildings. That includes the Comtesse. But her title, Julienne tells herself, is a barrier between her body and those of her servants. In addition, her reputation is spotless. And her kindness, a fortress behind which she takes refuge most of the time. No, surely the Comtesse cannot be suspected of having a love affair with André. But what of the others? And which of them? If she is no longer the only one, then what is she now? Are jealousy, pain, distress sufficient to believe one is still alive?

All emotion, all feeling weighs heavily on her.

She wishes she were dead.

92

The migraine will not leave him. It paralyzes him, nails him to his bed. Crucified on a raft that never sinks but drifts, and the drifting adds to his pain.

The Comtesse is there, by his bedside, every day.

Do not speak.

She dissolves a powder in a little water.

Drink.

He drinks.

The migraine does not give ground.

His skull is still in a vise.

He also feels as if he is floating.

Close your eyes.

He does not argue with her orders. With closed eyelids, he breathes in her scent with more intensity and becomes more sharply aware of the rustling of her dress, and it is as if a wave has suddenly struck him on the brow, as if his eyes were filled with the buzzing of a thousand wasps, it is torture, but he will not open his eyes.

Thank you.

93

She has begun addressing him more formally, as if he were her equal, just as she addresses her husband, her relations, her friends, those of her kind, and she has barely been aware of it.

Drink. Close your eyes. Sleep.

Julienne is present at all of the Comtesse's visits.

The Comtesse has stopped addressing him like a servant, Julienne has noticed it and since then has lost her wish to die. Jealous, that she is, very much so, and her jealousy has a target. Hate has taken possession of her, more powerfully than any man could ever do.

The Comtesse and her man are becoming closer, she sees that clearly now. Julienne lurks in a corner of the bedroom, unseen, forgotten by the two lovers, for that is what they are, how could she doubt it?

What is the name of the goddess of vengeance? Does she even have a name?

94

Since André has been an invalid, Sébastien has been promoted to head gardener, master of the flowers and the trees, the avenues and the honeysuckle-wreathed bridge over the artificial stream.

He misses André's voice, his glances, his shadow, their rare, fleeting embraces. But he grows accustomed to his absence. Sometimes he talks, to whom or what he does not know, telling their story, their love, his regret that he could not persuade his lover to venture with him out on the roads. And his dreams, what are they? Does suffering allow one to have dreams?

I would like to be a dream, and to visit you as a dream.

There is André and once again there is, very intensely, Balthazar, more intensely than yesterday or even than the old days, there is the Incomparable.

We are still one, you, Balthazar de Créon, and I. I thought you had left me, abandoned me, choose the word that suits you, my love, I thought I had turned away from you, I thought of what could not be.

95

At dusk, and on nights when there is a full moon, Sébastien wades in the cold water of the river, not the artificial one but the one beyond the grounds, that runs past the fields of corn and rye. It is not very deep. From it he gathers pebbles, the flattest smoothest ones he can find, and takes them back to his room, where he puts them in a trunk. Then he chooses from a previous harvest, and by the light of a candle paints his lover's mouth on the stone, or his chest, or his shoulders, or his penis, or his feet. He does not limit himself to resuscitating fragments of the beloved body. On one pebble, he has painted a cat rolled up like a turban, and on this other a beech tree, or a fully opened rose, or a hedge-lined path, or part of a hedge with a bird in its foliage, or a maid's cap, or the pendant with its glittering cross of diamonds the Comtesse always wears. He paints the world that is his, in small pieces, he paints whatever he likes. How many pebbles will he need to make an inventory of everything this world consists of? Myriads, no doubt.

His room is like a rockery.

He would kill anyone who, for fun, attempted to enter it.

96

And why not paint what is not but may yet happen?
What, for instance?
Well, the chateau in ruins, the scrub colonizing the banks of flowers, the grass invading the avenues, and the animals walking along them—stray dogs, cats and horses that have reverted to wildness, stags, foxes, wolves.

But no men or women.

Tonight he will get down to the task of depicting his vision.
Collapsed walls, brambles, wild animals.

97

He will bury them all. It is more than an intuition. Look at him, he has been dying for weeks and months, and still he is not dead. He seems outside time, barely human, who would recognize him, he is tough, a bag of bones mocking the Grim Reaper, he says neither yes nor no, he says, I don't give a damn about dying, I don't give a damn about living, while children are born, men and women die, time passes.

His endless death throes make him terrifying. He scares people. They cross themselves if they chance to pass the Francartins' lodge.

Only his wife and the Comtesse (what does she see in this dying man? Is there such a fine line between unfathomable pity and madness?) dare approach him and watch over him. They must seem like ghosts to him, or perhaps mothers, or sisters.

98

Yesterday, she caught the Comtesse becoming bolder—feeling his chest, stroking his hands and shoulder, whispering to him gently. Today is the same. They have been lovers, you would have to be blind not to see it.

She dares do that in front of my eyes. As if I didn't exist.

A dying man and a whore. A fine pair.

But between the two of them, she is still there, his wife, how can they forget her?

Lace. Silk. Satin. Cross of diamonds.

The Comtesse de C.

His lover.

In the chest, she finds an ax, a little ax, almost nothing.

99

Eyewitness, silent witness.
He was unable to get out of bed—like being stuck in pitch.
He saw the axe fall and the lady collapse, he heard the victim's silence, and the killer's.

He will hear that silence for a long time, until his death.

A death that does not come.

He sees the scene over and over, it lays waste to everything in him, wipes out everything, even the memory of his love for Sébastien.

A sharp sound of broken bones, a deafening noise, the last music he hears.

He asks his body to let go.

100

She was arrested six miles from the chateau, mumbling and disheveled, a senile witch, André's wife.

The Comtesse's funeral will take place tomorrow, it will be very grand, they say.

I will not paint that.

And in his bed, André was dead, and the look in his eyes, my God, what did you see?

No more death throes. The bed, the look in his eyes, and that is all.

I will not paint that.

The C. family will dismiss the servants and close the doors of the chateau. It is reluctant to live here, facing these grounds with their accursed little lodge.

I will not paint that.

I am here, Balthazar said. We will again be as one. But have we ever stopped being as one?

Be like me, he said to me, the prey of flames.

Do you not like flames?

I will not paint the fire. I will not paint my death.

But why paint them, my love? Why not accept the fire, why not accept death?

You are here, so close, almost body to body.

The curtain at my window catches fire, all it took was one candle, every fire starts from almost nothing, it is always thus, and the fire advances, it is on me, it embraces me, I am a torch, I collapse, and the fire sets everything ablaze, sets the world ablaze, and then I let go, I am dead.

ABOUT THE AUTHOR

Daniel Arsand was born in Avignon in 1950 and currently works as an editor with Édi-tions Phébus in Paris. He is the author of several novels, including *The Land of Dark-ness*, winner of the Prix Femina for First Fiction, and *In Silence*, winner of the Jean Giono Second Novel Grand Prix.

Europa Editions publishes in the USA and in the UK. Not all titles are available in both countries. Availability of individual titles is indicated in the following list.

Fiction

Carmine Abate
Between Two Seas • 978-1-933372-40-2 • Territories: World
The Homecoming Party • 978-1-933372-83-9 • Territories: World

Milena Agus
From the Land of the Moon • 978-1-60945-001-4 • Ebook • Territories: World (excl. ANZ)

Salwa Al Neimi
The Proof of the Honey • 978-1-933372-68-6 • Ebook • Territories: World (excl UK)

Simonetta Agnello Hornby
The Nun • 978-1-60945-062-5 • Territories: World

Daniel Arsand
Lovers • 978-1-60945-071-7 • Ebook • Territories: World

Jenn Ashworth
A Kind of Intimacy • 978-1-933372-86-0 • Territories: US & Can

Beryl Bainbridge
The Girl in the Polka Dot Dress • 978-1-60945-056-4 • Ebook • Territories: US

Muriel Barbery
The Elegance of the Hedgehog • 978-1-933372-60-0 • Ebook •
Territories: World (excl. UK & EU)
Gourmet Rhapsody • 978-1-933372-95-2 • Ebook • Territories:
World (excl. UK & EU)

Stefano Benni
Margherita Dolce Vita • 978-1-933372-20-4 • Territories: World
Timeskipper • 978-1-933372-44-0 • Territories: World

Romano Bilenchi
The Chill • 978-1-933372-90-7 • Territories: World

Kazimierz Brandys
Rondo • 978-1-60945-004-5 • Territories: World

Alina Bronsky
Broken Glass Park • 978-1-933372-96-9 • Ebook • Territories:
World
The Hottest Dishes of the Tartar Cuisine • 978-1-60945-006-9 •
Ebook • Territories: World

Jesse Browner
Everything Happens Today • 978-1-60945-051-9 • Ebook •
Territories: World (excl. UK & EU)

Francisco Coloane
Tierra del Fuego • 978-1-933372-63-1 • Ebook • Territories:
World

Rebecca Connell
The Art of Losing • 978-1-933372-78-5 • Territories: US

Laurence Cossé
A Novel Bookstore • 978-1-933372-82-2 • Ebook • Territories:
World
An Accident in August • 978-1-60945-049-6 • Territories: World
(excl. UK)

Diego De Silva
I Hadn't Understood • 978-1-60945-065-6 • Territories: World

Shashi Deshpande
The Dark Holds No Terrors • 978-1-933372-67-9 • Territories: US

Steve Erickson
Zeroville • 978-1-933372-39-6 • Territories: US & Can
These Dreams of You • 978-1-60945-063-2 • Territories: US & Can

Elena Ferrante
The Days of Abandonment • 978-1-933372-00-6 • Ebook •
Territories: World
Troubling Love • 978-1-933372-16-7 • Territories: World
The Lost Daughter • 978-1-933372-42-6 • Territories: World

Linda Ferri
Cecilia • 978-1-933372-87-7 • Territories: World

Damon Galgut
In a Strange Room • 978-1-60945-011-3 • Ebook • Territories: USA

Santiago Gamboa
Necropolis • 978-1-60945-073-1 • Ebook • Territories: World

Jane Gardam
Old Filth • 978-1-933372-13-6 • Ebook • Territories: US
The Queen of the Tambourine • 978-1-933372-36-5 • Ebook •
Territories: US
The People on Privilege Hill • 978-1-933372-56-3 • Ebook •
Territories: US
The Man in the Wooden Hat • 978-1-933372-89-1 • Ebook •
Territories: US
God on the Rocks • 978-1-933372-76-1 • Ebook • Territories: US
Crusoe's Daughter • 978-1-60945-069-4 • Ebook • Territories: US

Anna Gavalda
French Leave • 978-1-60945-005-2 • Ebook • Territories: US & Can

Seth Greenland
The Angry Buddhist • 978-1-60945-068-7 • Ebook • Territories:
World

Katharina Hacker
The Have-Nots • 978-1-933372-41-9 • Territories: World
(excl. India)

Patrick Hamilton
Hangover Square • 978-1-933372-06-8 • Territories: US & Can

James Hamilton-Paterson
Cooking with Fernet Branca • 978-1-933372-01-3 • Territories: US
Amazing Disgrace • 978-1-933372-19-8 • Territories: US
Rancid Pansies • 978-1-933372-62-4 • Territories: USA

Alfred Hayes
The Girl on the Via Flaminia • 978-1-933372-24-2 • Ebook •
Territories: World

Jean-Claude Izzo
The Lost Sailors • 978-1-933372-35-8 • Territories: World
A Sun for the Dying • 978-1-933372-59-4 • Territories: World

Gail Jones
Sorry • 978-1-933372-55-6 • Territories: US & Can

Ioanna Karystiani
The Jasmine Isle • 978-1-933372-10-5 • Territories: World
Swell • 978-1-933372-98-3 • Territories: World

Peter Kocan
Fresh Fields • 978-1-933372-29-7 • Territories: US, EU & Can
The Treatment and the Cure • 978-1-933372-45-7 • Territories:
US, EU & Can

Helmut Krausser
Eros • 978-1-933372-58-7 • Territories: World

Amara Lakhous
Clash of Civilizations Over an Elevator in Piazza Vittorio •
978-1-933372-61-7 • Ebook • Territories: World
Divorce Islamic Style • 978-1-60945-066-3 • Ebook • Territories:
World

Lia Levi
The Jewish Husband • 978-1-933372-93-8 • Territories: World

Valerio Massimo Manfredi
The Ides of March • 978-1-933372-99-0 • Territories: US

Leïla Marouane
The Sexual Life of an Islamist in Paris • 978-1-933372-85-3 •
Territories: World

Lorenzo Mediano
The Frost on His Shoulders • 978-1-60945-072-4 • Ebook •
Territories: World

Sélim Nassib
I Loved You for Your Voice • 978-1-933372-07-5 • Territories:
World
The Palestinian Lover • 978-1-933372-23-5 • Territories: World

Amélie Nothomb
Tokyo Fiancée • 978-1-933372-64-8 • Territories: US & Can
Hygiene and the Assassin • 978-1-933372-77-8 • Ebook •
Territories: US & Can

Valeria Parrella
For Grace Received • 978-1-933372-94-5 • Territories: World

Alessandro Piperno
The Worst Intentions • 978-1-933372-33-4 • Territories: World
Persecution • 978-1-60945-074-8 • Ebook • Territories: World

Lorcan Roche
The Companion • 978-1-933372-84-6 • Territories: World

Boualem Sansal
The German Mujahid • 978-1-933372-92-1 • Ebook •
Territories: US & Can

Eric-Emmanuel Schmitt
The Most Beautiful Book in the World • 978-1-933372-74-7 •
Ebook • Territories: World
The Woman with the Bouquet • 978-1-933372-81-5 • Ebook •
Territories: US & Can

Angelika Schrobsdorff
You Are Not Like Other Mothers • 978-1-60945-075-5 • Ebook
• Territories: World

Audrey Schulman
Three Weeks in December • 978-1-60945-064-9 • Ebook •
Territories: US & Can

James Scudamore
Heliopolis • 978-1-933372-73-0 • Ebook • Territories: US

Luis Sepúlveda
The Shadow of What We Were • 978-1-60945-002-1 • Ebook •
Territories: World

Paolo Sorrentino
Everybody's Right • 978-1-60945-052-6 • Ebook • Territories:
US & Can

Domenico Starnone
First Execution • 978-1-933372-66-2 • Territories: World

Henry Sutton
Get Me out of Here • 978-1-60945-007-6 • Ebook • Territories:
US & Can

Chad Taylor
Departure Lounge • 978-1-933372-09-9 • Territories: US, EU &
Can

Roma Tearne
Mosquito • 978-1-933372-57-0 • Territories: US & Can
Bone China • 978-1-933372-75-4 • Territories: US

www.europaeditions.com

André Carl van der Merwe
Moffie • 978-1-60945-050-2 • Ebook • Territories: World
(excl. S. Africa)

Fay Weldon
Chalcot Crescent • 978-1-933372-79-2 • Territories: US

Anne Wiazemsky
My Berlin Child • 978-1-60945-003-8 • Territories: US & Can

Jonathan Yardley
Second Reading • 978-1-60945-008-3 • Ebook • Territories: US
& Can

Edwin M. Yoder Jr.
Lions at Lamb House • 978-1-933372-34-1 • Territories: World

Michele Zackheim
Broken Colors • 978-1-933372-37-2 • Territories: World

Alice Zeniter
Take This Man • 978-1-60945-053-3 • Territories: World

Tonga Books

Ian Holding
Of Beasts and Beings • 978-1-60945-054-0 • Ebook • Territories:
US & Can

Sara Levine
Treasure Island!!! • 978-0-14043-768-3 • Ebook • Territories: World

Alexander Maksik
You Deserve Nothing • 978-1-60945-048-9 • Ebook • Territories: US, Can & EU (excl. UK)

Thad Ziolkowski
Wichita • 978-1-60945-070-0 • Ebook • Territories: World

Crime/Noir

Massimo Carlotto
The Goodbye Kiss • 978-1-933372-05-1 • Ebook • Territories: World
Death's Dark Abyss • 978-1-933372-18-1 • Ebook • Territories: World
The Fugitive • 978-1-933372-25-9 • Ebook • Territories: World
Bandit Love • 978-1-933372-80-8 • Ebook • Territories: World
Poisonville • 978-1-933372-91-4 • Ebook • Territories: World

Giancarlo De Cataldo
The Father and the Foreigner • 978-1-933372-72-3 • Territories: World

www.europaeditions.com

Caryl Férey
Zulu • 978-1-933372-88-4 • Ebook • Territories: World
(excl. UK & EU)
Utu • 978-1-60945-055-7 • Ebook • Territories: World
(excl. UK & EU)

Alicia Giménez-Bartlett
Dog Day • 978-1-933372-14-3 • Territories: US & Can
Prime Time Suspect • 978-1-933372-31-0 • Territories: US & Can
Death Rites • 978-1-933372-54-9 • Territories: US & Can

Jean-Claude Izzo
Total Chaos • 978-1-933372-04-4 • Territories: US & Can
Chourmo • 978-1-933372-17-4 • Territories: US & Can
Solea • 978-1-933372-30-3 • Territories: US & Can

Matthew F. Jones
Boot Tracks • 978-1-933372-11-2 • Territories: US & Can

Gene Kerrigan
The Midnight Choir • 978-1-933372-26-6 • Territories: US & Can
Little Criminals • 978-1-933372-43-3 • Territories: US & Can

Carlo Lucarelli
Carte Blanche • 978-1-933372-15-0 • Territories: World
The Damned Season • 978-1-933372-27-3 • Territories: World
Via delle Oche • 978-1-933372-53-2 • Territories: World

Edna Mazya
Love Burns • 978-1-933372-08-2 • Territories: World (excl. ANZ)

Yishai Sarid
Limassol • 978-1-60945-000-7 • Ebook • Territories: World
(excl. UK, AUS & India)

Joel Stone
The Jerusalem File • 978-1-933372-65-5 • Ebook • Territories:
World

Benjamin Tammuz
Minotaur • 978-1-933372-02-0 • Ebook • Territories: World

Non-fiction

Alberto Angela
A Day in the Life of Ancient Rome • 978-1-933372-71-6 •
Territories: World • History

Helmut Dubiel
Deep In the Brain: Living with Parkinson's Disease •
978-1-933372-70-9 • Ebook • Territories: World •
Medicine/Memoir

James Hamilton-Paterson
Seven-Tenths: The Sea and Its Thresholds • 978-1-933372-69-3 •
Territories: USA • Nature/Essays

www.europaeditions.com

Daniele Mastrogiacomo
Days of Fear • 978-1-933372-97-6 • Ebook • Territories: World
• Current affairs/Memoir/Afghanistan/Journalism

Valery Panyushkin
Twelve Who Don't Agree • 978-1-60945-010-6 • Ebook •
Territories: World • Current affairs/Memoir/Russia/Journalism

Christa Wolf
One Day a Year: 1960-2000 • 978-1-933372-22-8 • Territories:
World • Memoir/History/20th Century

Children's Illustrated Fiction

Altan
Here Comes Timpa • 978-1-933372-28-0 • Territories: World
(excl. Italy)
Timpa Goes to the Sea • 978-1-933372-32-7 • Territories: World
(excl. Italy)
Fairy Tale Timpa • 978-1-933372-38-9 • Territories: World
(excl. Italy)

Wolf Erlbruch
The Big Question • 978-1-933372-03-7 • Territories: US & Can
The Miracle of the Bears • 978-1-933372-21-1 • Territories: US
& Can
(with **Gioconda Belli**) *The Butterfly Workshop* •
978-1-933372-12-9 • Territories: US & Can